COLORFUL DREAMER

The Story of Artist Henri Matisse

Marjorie Blain Parker

illustrated by

Holly Berry

Dial Books for Young Readers

an imprint of Penguin Group (USA) Inc.

In memory of my grandmother Simone McDonald (née Madore), from whom I inherited the writing gene and who was French Canadian, to boot. She would have loved this book.
— M.B.P.

With love to Gwen . . . my colorful dreamer
— H.B.

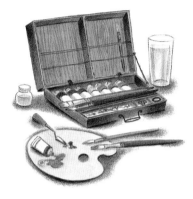

DIAL BOOKS FOR YOUNG READERS

A division of Penguin Young Readers Group · Published by The Penguin Group · Penguin Group (USA) Inc., 375 Hudson Street, New York, NY 10014, U.S.A. · Penguin Group (Canada), 90 Eglinton Avenue East, Suite 700, Toronto, Ontario, Canada M4P 2Y3 (a division of Pearson Penguin Canada Inc.) · Penguin Books Ltd, 80 Strand, London WC2R 0RL, England · Penguin Ireland, 25 St. Stephen's Green, Dublin 2, Ireland (a division of Penguin Books Ltd) · Penguin Group (Australia), 250 Camberwell Road, Camberwell, Victoria 3124, Australia (a division of Pearson Australia Group Pty Ltd) · Penguin Books India Pvt Ltd, 11 Community Centre, Panchsheel Park, New Delhi - 110 017, India · Penguin Group (NZ), 67 Apollo Drive, Rosedale, Auckland 0632, New Zealand (a division of Pearson New Zealand Ltd) · Penguin Books (South Africa) (Pty) Ltd, 24 Sturdee Avenue, Rosebank, Johannesburg 2196, South Africa · Penguin Books Ltd, Registered Offices: 80 Strand, London WC2R 0RL, England

Designed by Mina Chung · Text set in Lomba · Manufactured in China on acid-free paper
10 9 8 7 6 5 4 3 2 1

Library of Congress Cataloging-in-Publication Data
Parker, Marjorie Blain.
Colorful dreamer : the story of artist Henri Matisse / Marjorie Blain Parker ; illustrated by Holly Berry.
p. cm.
ISBN 978-0-8037-3758-7 (hardcover)
1. Matisse, Henri, 1869–1954—Juvenile literature. 2. Artists—France—Biography—Juvenile literature.
I. Matisse, Henri, 1869–1954. II. Berry, Holly. III. Title.
N6853.M33P37 2012 759.4—dc23 [B] 2011035446

JP
PARKER

This art was created using colored pencils, acrylic paint, watercolor, ink, and collage on rag paper.

Years ago a dreamy boy gazed out his bedroom window. He lived in a dreary village in France. It was an industrial town—choked with factories, clanking looms, and smoking chimneys.

There were no gardens to wander, no museums to visit, no paintings to admire.

But even in this muddy, smudgy place there were violets and butterflies in spring. There were fairs and circuses in summer. There were brilliant fabrics in every weaver's house.

And the boy's dreams were full of color.

His name was Henri.

Henri's parents loved him very much. But, sometimes, they worried about him. They worried he might end up down-and-out. Life was difficult. They worked so hard to make a decent living. And Henri was not a hard worker.

He did not excel at school.

He did not excel at violin lessons.

He did not, in fact, excel at much of anything—except, perhaps, dreaming.

Henri dreamed of a colorful and exciting life.

He dreamed of being a clown or an acrobat in a traveling show.

He dreamed of being an actor or a magician on stage.

Henri dreamed of being noticed.

He did *not* dream of taking over his parents' store. Just thinking about it tied his stomach in knots. And talking to his father about it could send Henri to bed for a week.

By the time Henri was a young man, his parents decided that his brother should take over the family business. And, to their great relief, Henri agreed to study law in Paris.

Perhaps their oldest son would not end up down-and-out after all.

It certainly wasn't the life Henri had dreamed about. Law clerks, he discovered, spent long days copying legal documents, word-for-word-for-word. When he couldn't stand the boredom for another second, Henri amused himself with his peashooter. Soon, he was an excellent shot!

Growing a beard and wearing a top hat didn't help. Though he looked like a law clerk, Henri couldn't bear the possibility of such an existence. Just thinking about it tied his stomach in knots. And this time Henri ended up in bed for *months*—in a hospital.

Poor Henri—being stuck in bed was almost worse than his job. He noticed that the man next to him kept cheerfully busy by painting small landscapes.

At least it would be something to do, thought Henri. So he asked if his mother would buy him a set of paints.

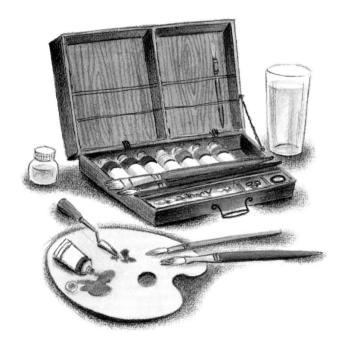

The moment Henri opened that box, he knew. The colors! *This* was what he had been dreaming of.

He picked up the paintbrush and was transported into paradise.

Henri painted in the hospital until he was healthy enough to leave.

He painted in the morning before he went to work.

He painted during his lunch break.

He painted in the evening after he got home from work.

Henri even drew on the documents he was supposed to be copying while he was *at* work.

It was clear he was never going to be a lawyer.

Henri's parents were horrified. To be an artist meant catastrophe. It was as bad as being a clown or an acrobat. It was as bad as being an actor or a magician. Henri *would* end up down-and-out. They would have to support him for the rest of his life or he would starve.

But Henri *was* a hard worker after all.

He studied and practiced and experimented.

He excelled at art school.

Henri learned how to play the violin. He loved the music—how it calmed his nerves and exercised his hands. He learned to play it very, very well.

Henri excelled at many things.

It wasn't easy. For years he *was* hungry—very hungry. For years he struggled to provide for his family.

But Henri was stubborn. He refused to give up.

He dreamed colorful dreams. He painted colorful paintings. And, little by little, people noticed.

Henri crisscrossed the globe—to Algeria, Morocco, Tahiti, Italy, America—and painted.

He moved to the coast, where the light was clear and the colors bright. He named his villa "Le Reve"—the Dream—and he filled it with birds and goldfish and flowers and fabrics. Here too he painted, as more and more people noticed.

Henri kept painting and years kept passing until, white-haired and sick, he found himself back where he had started—in bed.

Too weak to stand at an easel, he made cut-out collages instead. By now the brilliant colors were too bright for his old eyes. But that didn't stop Henri. He simply wore sunglasses in his bedroom!

Henri "painted" with colored paper. He called it "drawing with scissors."

And these were among his greatest creations.
Henri was unstoppable.
He worked as hard as any artist ever had.
He worked until the very day he died.

And, by then, the whole world had noticed

Henri Matisse.

A Note about Henri Matisse

Henri Matisse was born on New Year's Eve 1869, in northern France. Although he once won an award at school for drawing, Matisse did not discover painting until he was twenty, at which point it became his lifelong passion. Throughout the next sixty-five years, Matisse explored and experimented with different themes, styles, and mediums. There were many ups and downs: He experienced poverty, especially as an art student, but also after he was married with a family. And, at first, Matisse's work was laughed at. Art critics sneered at his canvases, considering his techniques shocking—the use of green in a woman's face, for example. They called him a *Fauve*, which is French for "wild beast." But, luckily, some collectors recognized Matisse's extraordinary talent and became patrons. They bought his paintings, providing both financial support and creative encouragement.

Matisse was very interested in the human figure, painting people (especially women) much more frequently than landscapes or still lifes. And, always, there was a lot of color! Many of Matisse's paintings feature bright flowers, or dazzling goldfish, or vivid and intricate fabrics. The paper cutouts he created when he was older are celebrated for their fresh brilliance and their playful simplicity. Known as "the master of color," Matisse ultimately became one of the most famous artists in the world.

In addition to his paintings and paper cutouts, Matisse also drew, sculpted, and was an accomplished printmaker. He even, toward the end of his life, designed a chapel—from the architecture to the stained glass, furniture, decorations, and even the vestments (priests' robes). He considered it his masterpiece. Confined to a wheelchair, and then to bed, in his last years, Matisse refused to give up—cutting paper when he could no longer paint; attaching sticks of charcoal to long poles so he could draw on the walls. Matisse died of a heart attack in 1954, at the age of eighty-four, just two days after he had completed what was to be his final work. No doubt he already had plans for the next project!

For more information, you might enjoy:
Henri Matisse: Drawing with Scissors by Jane O'Connor, Grosset & Dunlap, 2002
Henri Matisse (Artists in Their Time series) by Jude Welton, Franklin Watts, 2002

Artwork by Matisse is on display at the following museums:

The Museum of Modern Art (MOMA), New York	The San Francisco Museum of Modern Art (SFMOMA)
The Metropolitan Museum, New York	The National Gallery of Canada, Ottawa, Ontario
The Art Institute of Chicago	Le Musée Matisse, Nice, France
The Baltimore Museum of Art (BMA): The Cone Collection	La Chapelle de Vence, Vence, France
The National Gallery of Art, Washington, DC	Le Musée d'Art Moderne, Paris, France
The Barnes Foundation, Philadelphia	The Hermitage Museum, St. Petersburg, Russia
The Carnegie Museum of Art, Pittsburgh	The Pushkin Museum of Fine Arts, Moscow, Russia